Our Weather

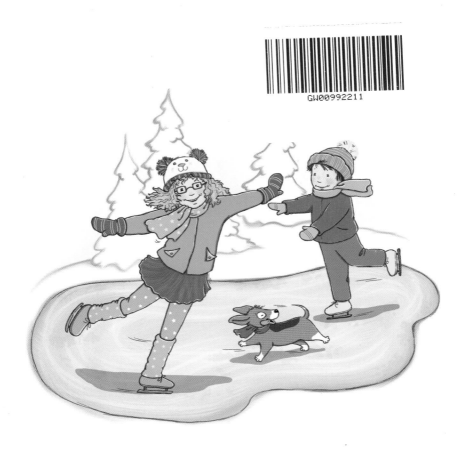

written by Pam Holden
illustrated by Deborah C. Johnson

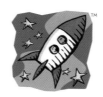

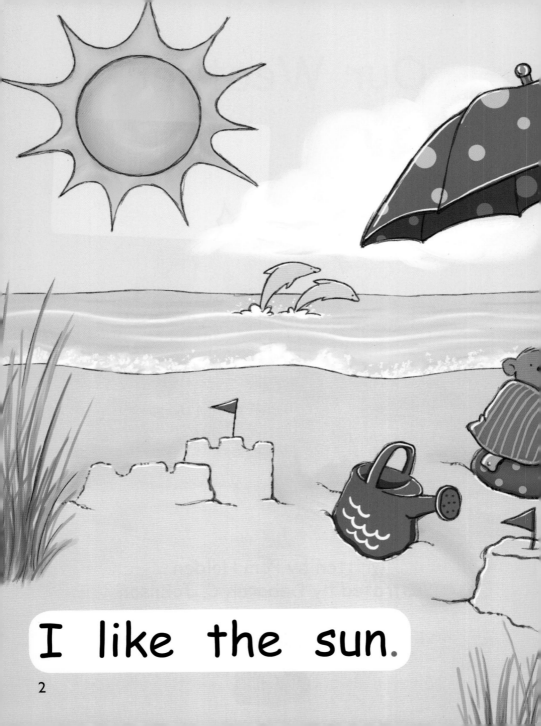

I like the sun.

2

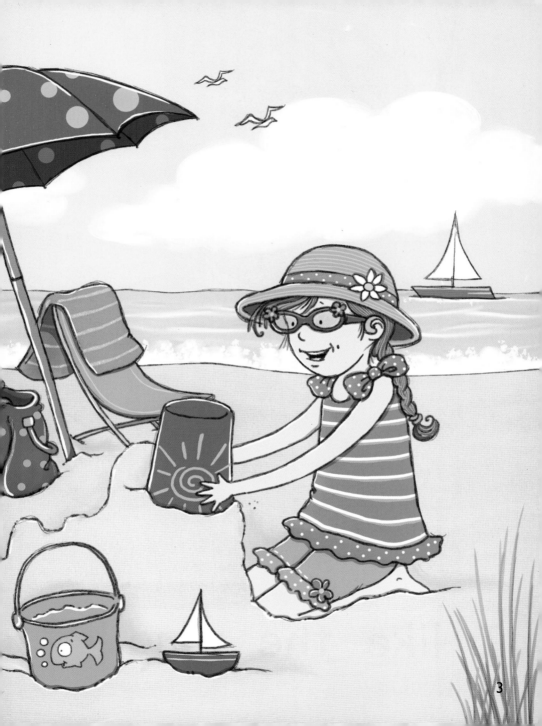

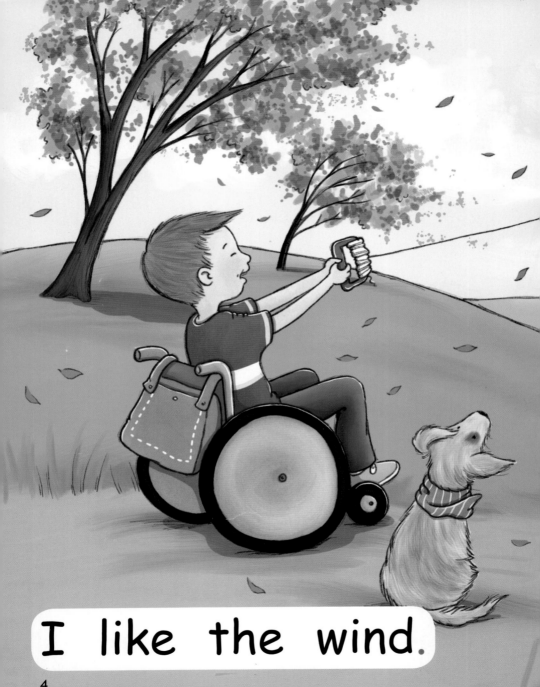

I like the wind.

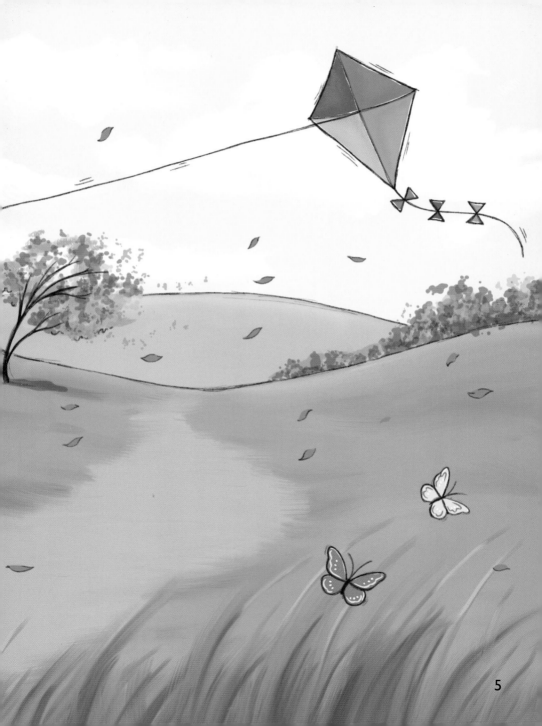

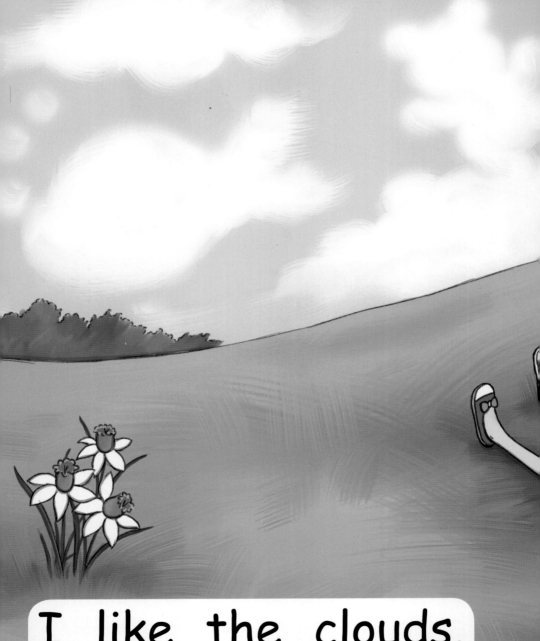

I like the clouds.

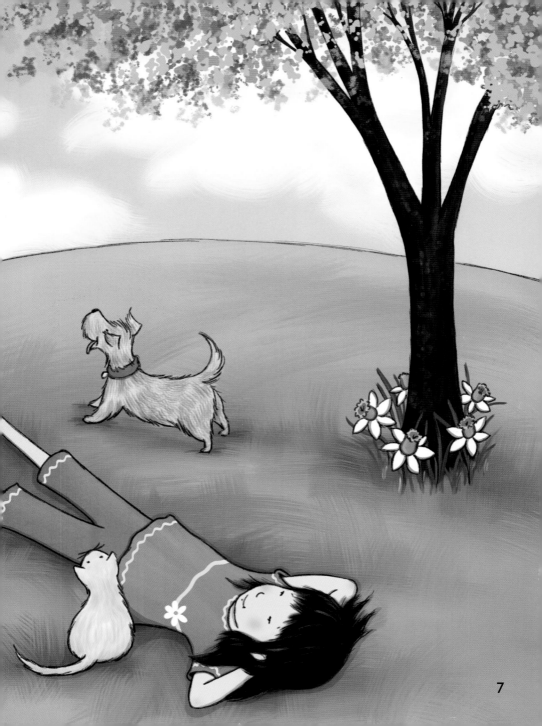

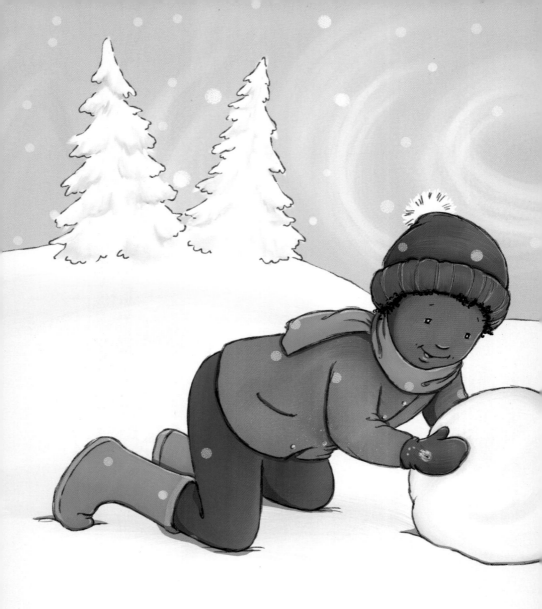

I like the snow.

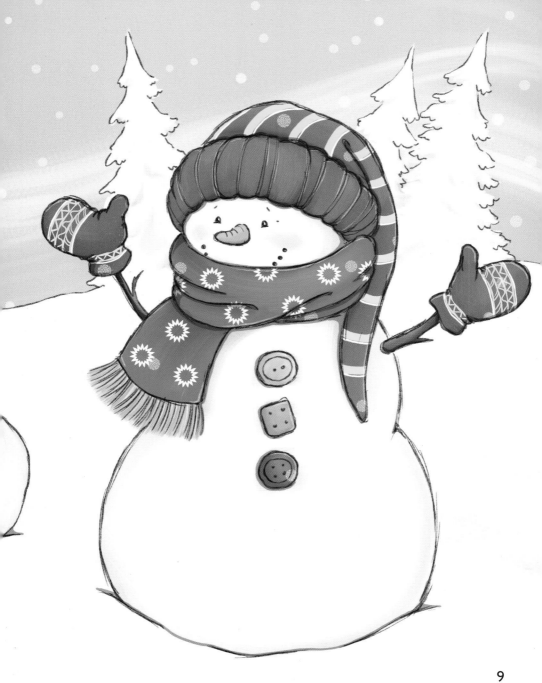

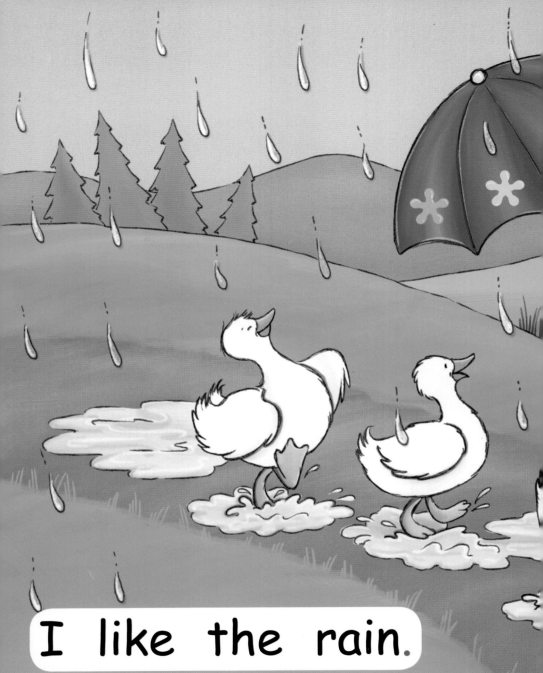

I like the rain.

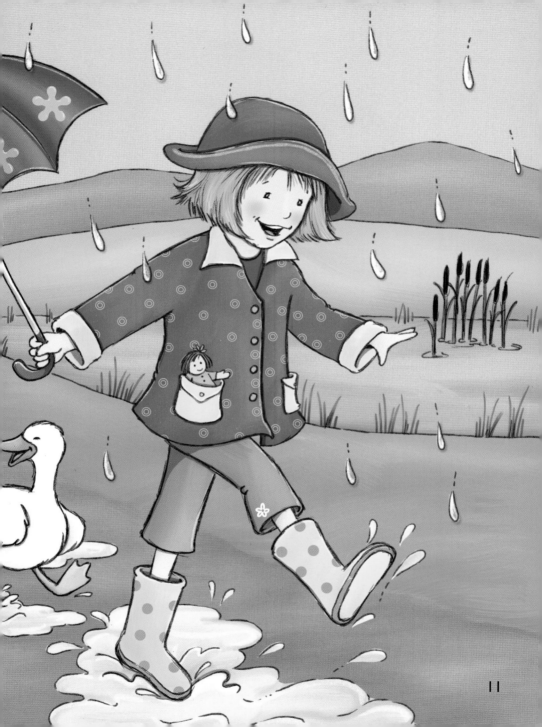

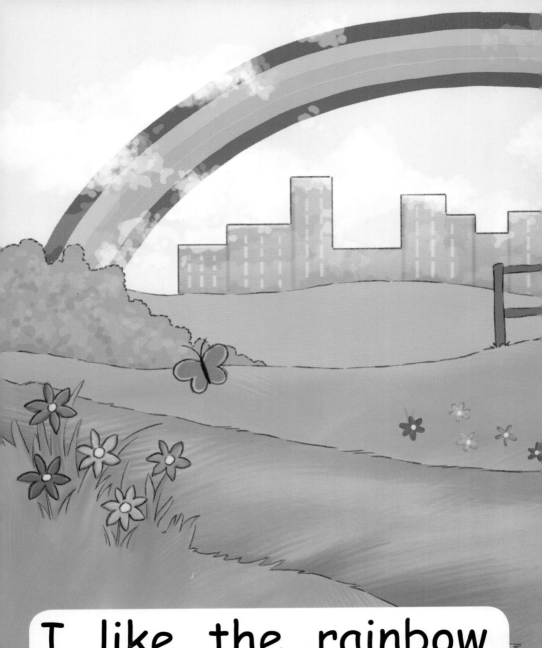

I like the rainbow.

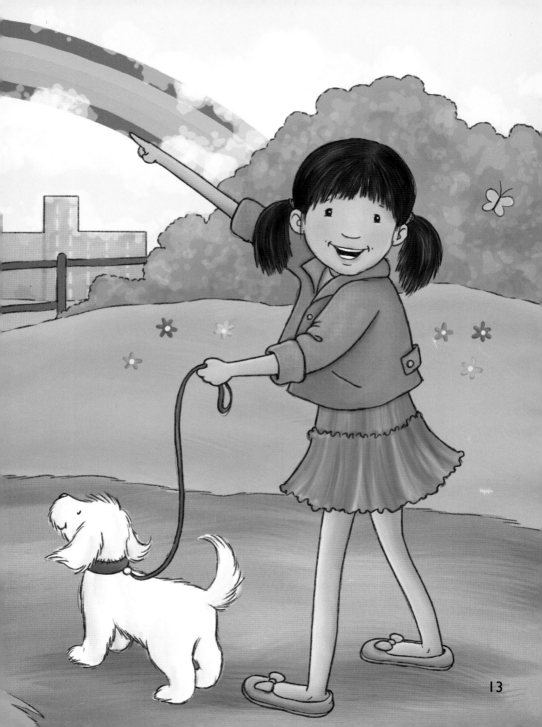

13

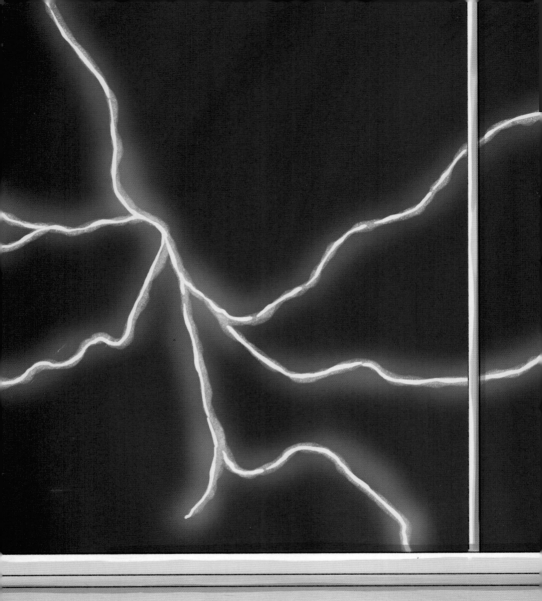

I like the lightning.

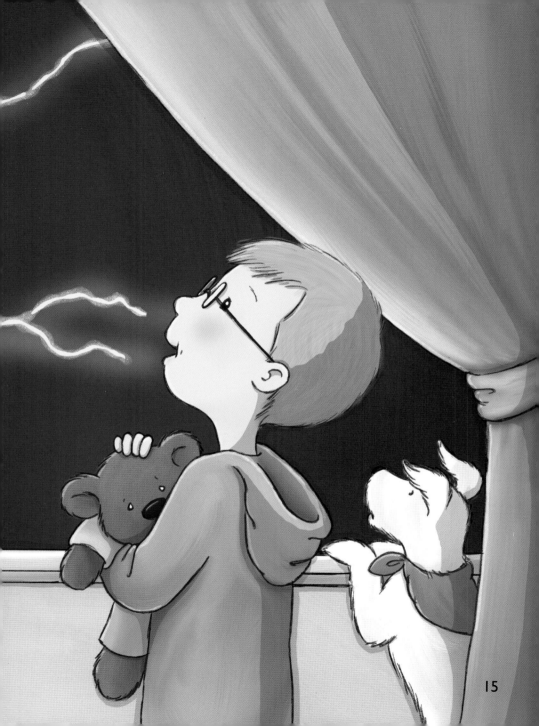

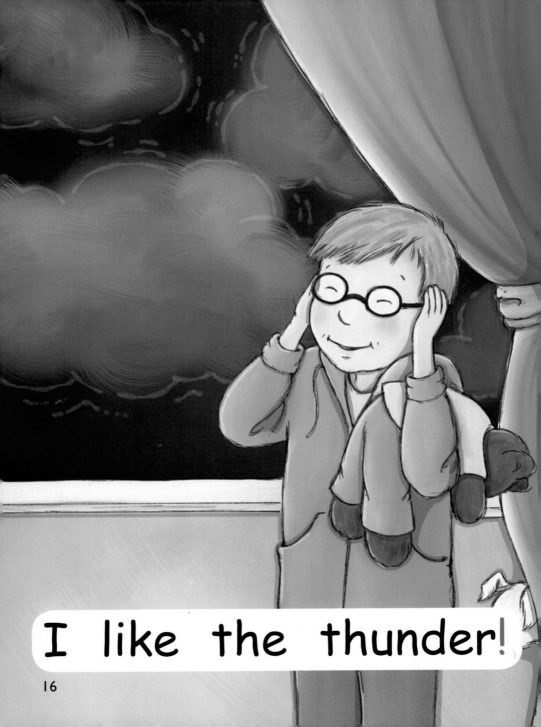

I like the thunder!